W9-CBM-818

Mop Top

For Chipper and Daryl,

Michael and Diane,

Ethan and Sean,

Jeff and Roy,

and all red-haired topknotters

everywhere

MOP TOP

Puffin Books

PUFFIN BOOKS

Published by the Penguin Group

Penguin Putnam Books for Young Readers,

345 Hudson Street, New York, New York 10014, U.S.A.

Penguin Books Ltd, 27 Wrights Lane, London W8 5TZ, England

Penguin Books Australia Ltd, Ringwood, Victoria, Australia

Penguin Books Canada Ltd, 10 Alcorn Avenue, Toronto, Ontario, Canada M4V 3B2

Penguin Books (N.Z.) Ltd, 182-190 Wairau Road, Auckland 10, New Zealand

Penguin Books Ltd, Registered Offices: Harmondsworth, Middlesex, England

First published by the Viking Press 1955
Viking Seafarer edition published 1970
Reprinted in 1972, 1974
Published in Picture Puffins 1978

29 27 25   24 26 28 30

Library of Congress Cataloging in Publication Data
Freeman, Don   Mop top.
Summary: An almost-six-year-old with a mass of floppy red hair
tries to postpone the inevitable trip to Mr. Barberoli's barber shop.
[1. Hair—Care and hygiene—Fiction]   I. Title.
[PZ7.F8747Mo   1978]   [E]   78-11246
ISBN-13: 978-0-14-050326-5

Set in Bodoni Bold

This is the story of a boy who never wanted to have his hair cut.

Everybody called him Moppy, because on top he looked like a floppy red mop.

8

Moppy didn't care what anybody said about his hair or what they called him. All he wanted was to stay at home and play.

9

He sometimes played at being a soaring eagle,

and he sometimes played at being a roaring lion. A good
lion he made too, without even trying!

11

But the time came when something had to be done about
Moppy's top. And it happened one day when he was swing-
ing from branch to branch in his very own chinaberry tree.

12

His mother came out into the garden and said, "Pardon me, but just who do you think you are up there—Tarzan?"

"Oh no, Mother, I'm not Tarzan!" said Moppy. " I'm a man from Mars, and I'm visiting all the stars and other planets!"

"Well then, Mister Man-from-Mars, could you plan to make a landing on this earth sometime today? We want you to hop to the barbershop and get that floppy mop clipped off before your birthday party tomorrow."

The minute Moppy heard the words "birthday party" he dropped down out of the tree to the ground, feet first, then stretched out his hand.

"Here's some money, sonny," his mother said. "I've just called Mister Barberoli, and he says he'll be ready for you at four o'clock sharp. It's a little after half-past three now, so let's see you hippity-hop to the barbershop all by yourself."

17

Moppy put the money in his pocket, and off he zoomed
across the vacant lot, like a rocket to the moon.

But just as soon as he turned the corner he slowed down
to a trot.

"Don't need my hair cut at all—anyway not now," he grumbled, and stumbled along until some bright red lollipops in a candy-store window caught his eye. They looked so good he had to stop.

While he stood there staring, what should waddle up but
a frilly woolly pup.

"What a silly-looking pup you are!" said Moppy as he bent down and tried to find the pup's eyes. "You're the one who needs a haircut, not me!"

And then they both trotted away in opposite directions.

Moppy hadn't gone very far before he saw Mr. Lawson mowing his lawn.

"That lawn is what needs a haircut, not me!" said Moppy.

25

Mr. Lawson stopped to wipe his brow and said, "How about letting me use this machine on that grassy patch of yours, boy? It could do with a little mowing."

26

Moppy thought he ought to get going, so off he hopped.

But the closer he got to the barbershop, the slower he hopped.

He was nearly there when he saw a man on a ladder, snipping branches off a low, droopy tree.

"Maybe a tree needs a clipping, but not me!" said Moppy.

29

"Oh, I don't know about that," said the man on the ladder.
"You could do with a few snips of these snippers, skipper!"

At that Moppy skipped away and came at last to the barbershop.

But hard as he tried, he could not go inside!

He decided to run and hide in the grocery store next
door, where he could think things over.

And this is where he hid—behind a barrel of brooms and brushes and fancy red mops!

By and by a lady without her glasses came up and told the salesman she wanted a mop to help her keep her kitchen floor clean.

"What's more, I want the strongest, fluffiest, floppiest mop you have in the store, sir," she said as she began shaking the mops, one at a time.

"Here, this one will do very well," said the lady. "I'll take
it along with me right now."

"Ouch! Let go!" shouted Moppy. "I'm not a mop! I'm a boy!"

The lady certainly did let go, and in a hurry too, as Moppy
scurried out the door and headed straight for Mister Barberoli's barbershop!

39

"I thought maybe you forgot," said roly-poly Mister Barberoli. "But you're right on the dot. It's exactly four!" Then
in one long leap Moppy was up on the barber-chair seat
ready to get his hair cut nice and neat.

40

"Please, Mister Barberoli, don't let me look like a mop any more," pleaded Moppy. "I don't want to clean anybody's kitchen floor!"

In a jiffy Mister Barberoli was clipping and snipping away, and combing and cropping without once stopping, as if he hadn't a minute to lose.

Finally he did stop. He held up a mirror and said, "Well, sonny, who's that, would you say?"

"It's me! It's me without that floppy old mop on top! Hooray!" said the boy in the chair.

Then he hopped down and gave Mister Barberoli the money. And out the door he flew, light as a feather.

All the world looked spick-and-span, as the boy who was
once called Moppy hopped up the street for home.

Everything felt new now, even the weather! The tree was
neat and tidy. The lawn was nicely mowed.
And look at the pup! Even he's had a trim!

Next day at his Birthday Party there was a beautiful big cake with six candles lit, and on the frosting was written:

HAPPY BIRTHDAY TO MARTY!

which was his real and true name all the time
and forevermore!